ALEXANDER AND THE BLUE GHOST

Written and illustrated by Osamu Nishikawa

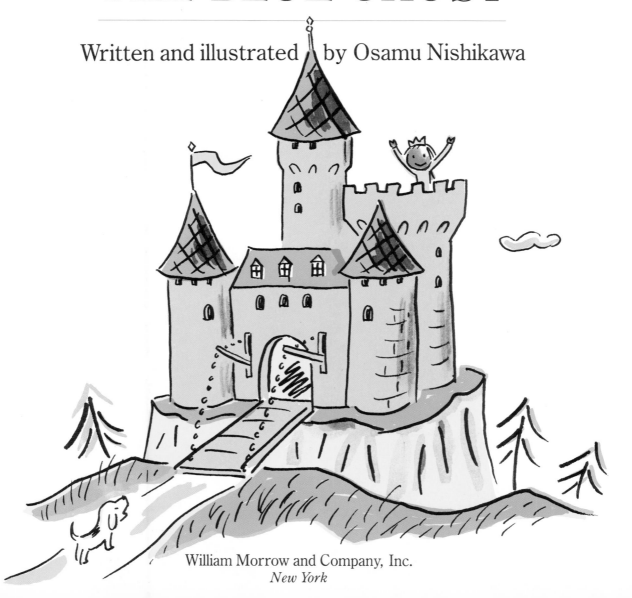

William Morrow and Company, Inc.
New York

Printed in the United States of America.   1 2 3 4 5 6 7 8 9 10
LC Card Number 86-5413
ISBN 0-688-06266-0   ISBN 0-688-06267-9 (lib. bdg.)

The king and queen always read a story to Prince Alexander before bedtime. One evening, as she closed the book, the queen said to Alexander, "Your father and I leave tomorrow to attend an important conference across the sea. We wish we didn't have to leave you, but I am afraid we must."

"You, of course, will be in charge of the kingdom," said the king.

"And your favorite uncle, Sir Bertrand, will be in charge of you," said the queen, giving Alexander an enormous hug.

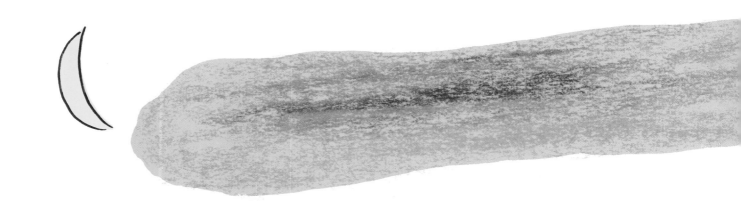

No sooner had the king and queen left than the castle was attacked by soldiers from a neighboring country.

A careless guard had left the drawbridge down. With a mighty roar, the invaders rushed inside the castle . . .

and quickly captured everyone they could find.

Sir Bertrand bravely protected his young nephew. Trixie, the royal dog, barked fiercely.

Sir Bertrand was wounded! As he collapsed, he gasped,
"Run... Alexander... to the tower! Be quick!"

There was no place to hide in the cold tower room. By the light of a flickering torch, Prince Alexander watched the mice play among the dusty cannonballs and listened for the invaders' footsteps.

What will become of me if I am captured? Alexander asked himself. He thought of his parents and wondered if he would ever see them again.

The soldiers were almost upon him, and Alexander knew he had to save himself and the kingdom.

"This is our only chance," he explained to Trixie. What if the cannon didn't work? What if it backfired? Alexander closed his eyes as he held out the torch.

BOOOOM!

From out of the smoke, a blue object filled the tower room.
"Attack our prince, will you?" it shrieked, swooping down on the
terrified soldiers.

"Go back where you belong!" thundered the blue ghost. It chased the soldiers out of the castle, through the kingdom, and over the border to their own country. The soldiers ran all the way with Trixie barking at their heels.

"How can I ever thank you?" asked Prince Alexander when the ghost and Trixie returned.

"I was glad to do it," said the ghost. "But now let us pay your neighbors a visit and see how much *they* like being invaded." The ghost slithered into the cannon and motioned for Alexander to climb on his back.

Off they went. From the balcony, Trixie barked.

The blue ghost flew directly to the neighboring king's palace.
Ghost and prince were bombarded with arrows. At first, Alexander
was frightened, but when he saw how the ghost returned the arrows,
he shouted, "Yah, yah, take that...and that," and watched the
enemy soldiers rushing around the castle walls in confusion.

"Help! Earthquake!" shouted the terrified soldiers in the tower. When they saw it was a ghost and not an earthquake at all, they threw down their bows and arrows and surrendered.

"Let us out of here," they begged.

"Oh, all right," said the ghost. He had other things to do.

Outside a castle window, Prince Alexander and the ghost waited until the king passed by. Then the ghost stuck out his long, wet tongue and gently tickled the king. The king giggled. The ghost tickled some more and soon the king was laughing so hard he fell into the arms of his guards.

"Stop! My stomach hurts," gasped the king. "This isn't funny."
"Will you keep the peace from now on?" asked the ghost sternly.
"Yes, yes, yes, I promise," said the king. "Now go away, please."
Alexander climbed onto the blue ghost's back, and they set off for
home.

Trixie was the first to greet them. Prince Alexander and the blue
ghost were heroes.

Alexander reported to Sir Bertrand, who was confined to his bed recovering from the wound he had received on the tower step.

"Your parents would want you to knight the blue ghost," Sir Bertrand told Alexander.

"But I haven't a sword," said Alexander.

"Borrow mine," said Sir Bertrand. "I'm only sorry I can't be there."

At the ceremony, Trixie was given a bone as a reward for her bravery.

From that time on, the blue knight seldom left Alexander's side. He and Trixie were Alexander's most faithful friends. It was the blue knight who read to Alexander at bedtime until the king and queen returned.

"Thank you for saving our child and our kingdom, Sir Ghost," said the royal couple upon their return. To show their gratitude the king and queen arranged for the blue knight to have a soft bed next to Alexander's. The blue knight did not tell anyone he was not comfortable in it.

Every once in a while, for old time's sake, he returned to the tower room, and there he had a good night's rest in his cozy old cannon. Alexander never knew, but even if he had, he wouldn't have minded.